From the award-winning
www.FunnyStatus.Com

FUNNY
STATUS UPDATES
for
FACEBOOK

From the award-winning
www.FunnyStatus.Com

FUNNY
STATUS UPDATES
for
FACEBOOK

ERIK GROSET

Advantage®

Published by Advantage, Charleston, South Carolina.
Member of Advantage Media Group.

ADVANTAGE is a registered trademark and the Advantage colophon is a trademark of Advantage Media Group, Inc.

Printed in the United States of America.

ISBN: 978-159932-326-8
LCCN: 2012937988

This publication is designed to provide accurate and authoritative information in regard to the subject matter covered. It is sold with the understanding that the publisher is not engaged in rendering legal, accounting, or other professional services. If legal advice or other expert assistance is required, the services of a competent professional person should be sought.

PREFACE

Did you know the average person checks Facebook over six times a day? Odds are, you probably check it even more than that. The Facebook social network allows us to express ourselves in ways we never could have imagined before.

Now, we can communicate instantly with our friends, family, and even complete strangers, in a new, magical, socially acceptable fashion.

The goal of this book is to inform you of some of the hottest trends on Facebook. It is intended to bring spice to your daily status updates and spread joy across your personal or organization's social network. My hope is for overall funnier status updates!

About Facebook

Founded in 2004, Facebook's mission is to make the world more open and connected. People use Facebook to stay connected with friends and family, to discover what's going on in the world, and to share and express what matters to them.

Q: Did you know?

A: You can also access Facebook by going to FB.com!

Facebook Stats

- ☞ Today, there are more than 845 million active users.
- ☞ 50% of active users log on to Facebook in any given day.
- ☞ More than 50 million users update their status each day.
- ☞ More than 60 million status updates posted each day.
- ☞ More than 3 billion photos uploaded to the site each month.

- More than 5 billion pieces of content (web links, news stories, blog posts, notes, photo albums, etc.) shared each week.
- More than 3.5 million events created each month.
- More than 3 million active Pages on Facebook.
- More than 1.5 million local businesses have active Pages on Facebook.
- More than 20 million people become fans of Pages each day.
- Pages have created more than 5.3 billion fans.

Average User

- Average user has 150 friends on the site.
- Average user sends 8 friend requests per month.
- Average user spends more than 55 minutes per day on Facebook.
- Average user clicks the Like button on 9 pieces of content each month.
- Average user writes 25 comments on Facebook content each month.

- Average user becomes a fan of 4 Pages each month
- Average user is invited to 3 events per month.
- Average user is a member of 13 groups.

International Growth

- More than 70 translations available on the site.
- About 80% of Facebook users are outside the U.S.
- Over 300,000 users helped translate the site through the translations application.

Platform

- More than 1 million developers and entrepreneurs from more than 180 countries.
- Every month, more than 70% of Facebook users engage with Platform applications.
- More than 500,000 active applications currently on Facebook Platform.
- More than 250 applications have more than 1 million monthly active users.

- ☞ More than 80,000 websites have implemented Facebook Connect since its general availability in December 2008.
- ☞ More than 60 million Facebook users engage with Facebook Connect on external websites every month.
- ☞ Two-thirds of comScore's U.S. Top 100 websites and half of comScore's Global Top 100 websites have implemented Facebook Connect.

Mobile

- ☞ There are more than 100 million active users currently accessing Facebook through their mobile devices.
- ☞ People that use Facebook on their mobile devices are twice as active on Facebook than non-mobile users.
- ☞ There are more than 200 mobile operators in 60 countries working to deploy and promote Facebook mobile products.

Facebook Stats Source: http://www.newsroom.fb.com

1 in every 2 Americans has a Facebook Profile

Source: http://techcrunch.com/2011/07/22/more-americans-are-on-facebook-than-have-a-passport/

Now That's Disgusting!

Facebook has been linked to a resurgence in the sexually-transmitted disease syphilis, according to health experts.

Source: http://www.telegraph.co.uk/technology/Facebook/7508945/Facebook-linked-to-rise-in-syphillis.html

PART I
TOP STATUSES

Get more LIKEs per status

Creating a Memorable Top Status Update

A large portion of this book is dedicated to giving examples of amazing statuses for every occasion. Most of these have been strategically chosen because they are "Top" statuses, meaning they've received thousands of LIKEs and/or comments per post. Although there is no magical formula that will give you a Top Status, we can help highlight what makes a killer status!

Did You Know?
If you press "L" while looking at a picture on Facebook, that you'll LIKE it?

What Makes a Top Status Update?

Good News! You *too* can make a top status update.

That's right. It isn't as hard as you think. Making a memorable status is actually pretty simple. You just have to be smart!

Try using an old salesman technique. Ask yourself...

"What does this status have to offer for the people who read it?"

Example:

Bad Status: Heading out to the gym tonight.

Good Status: Nutrition facts are useless, just tell me how long I have to be at the gym if I eat this.

Which Statuses Get the Most LIKEs?

- ☞ **Funny Status Updates** - Be witty and get rewarded.
- ☞ **Relevant/Topical** - Talk about recent events.
- ☞ **Multimedia** - Music, Movies, TV Shows, Pop-Culture.
- ☞ **Opinionated** - Taking one side or another on a hot topic.
- ☞ **Involvement** - Asking questions or asking people for their opinions or LIKEs.

Other ideas:

- ☞ **Pets** - People love hearing adorable stories about pets.

- ☞ **Food** - If there's one thing people love, it's food.
- ☞ **Babies** - Just like pets, they're undeniably adorable especially when they sing, dance, or cuddle with a puppy.
- ☞ **Politics** - What pisses you off? Talk about it!

ANTI-TOP STATUSES:*

- ☞ **Everyday Life** - Leave that boringness for Twitter. Nobody cares if you just hit the restroom.
- ☞ **Your Job Sucks** - So does everyone's. Stop being negative.

* If you post about these topics, you may have to delete your status in shame.

Memorable Statuses

Congratulations, now you know a little bit about creating a memorable status update! This should help reduce your awkwardly having to erase your boring unoriginal status when it hasn't been given any attention within 5 minutes. Don't kid yourself; we've all been there!

The good news is that you're well on your way to getting more LIKEs and comments per status.

The bad news is you've got lots more to learn!

To create a memorable status update is to condense paragraphs of wit into a lovable one or two-liner.

Did you know?
The average person gets 2 LIKEs per status.

That, my friends, is just embarrassing. It doesn't have to be like this! We can help your inner status-genius come out and show itself. After applying our ideas, suggestions, and apps—people average around 9.4 **LIKEs** per status. So, listen up!

Dos & Don'ts of Top Statuses

Do...

- ☞ Be creative and witty.
- ☞ Think about what works!
- ☞ Consider if you'd LIKE this status.
- ☞ Get input from someone else on what they think of your status.
- ☞ Use spell check!

Don't...

- ☞ Post random irrelevant song lyrics.
- ☞ Choose a boring quote from a website.
- ☞ Embarrass yourself - use proper grammar!
- ☞ Be vague, so that only you understand what you're saying.
- ☞ Use just a "single" word.

Keep in mind that your status updates and tweets become part of a permanent record. You don't want people to read your unintelligible rambles and thoughtless garbage years later, do you? We didn't think so! Now's the time to get cranking and become a master of crafting quality top statuses!

TOP STATUS UPDATES

Top 25 Status Updates of 2012

1. LIKE IF you put things in a safe place and then forget where the safe place is ☺

2. Did you know? It's impossible to say "Good Eye Might" without sounding Australian? LIKE if you tried!

3. LIKE if you have 50 t-shirts, but you only wear 7 of them and complain that you have no clothes.

4. The awkward moment when you're at your friend's house and your friend

is getting yelled at, so you just stand there and pet the dog.

5. Our phones fall, we panic. Our friends fall, we laugh.

6. fri(END], boyfri(END], girlfri(END]. Everything has an END, exept for fam(ILY].

7. 3 things I want in a relationship: Eyes that wont cry, lips than wont lie, and love that wont die. ♥

8. That awkward moment when sarcasm doesn't work in a text.

9. Facebook should have a limit on times you can update your relationship status, after 3 it should default to "unstable."

10. Our generation is going to have the weirdest grandparents ever. Tatted, pierced up, and listening to rap. Grandma got a lip ring yo!

11. Common sense is so rare it should be classified as a super power.

12. A relationship with no trust is like a cell phone with no service. All you can do is play games.

13. Facebook says we're "friends" but, trust me, I wouldn't hesitate to punch you in the face.

14. Dear life. When I asked if my day could get worse it was a rhetorical question not a challenge.

15. Yes, I end a Facebook conversation by hitting the (LIKE) button on the last comment.

16. The awkward moment when you've already said "what?" three times and still have no idea what the person said, so you just agree.

17. Hey, I found your nose; it was in my business again.

18. That awkward moment when the guy who discovered milk had to explain what he was doing to the cow.

19. Pick a number, double it, add 10, and divide it by 2, then minus it by the number you started with. LIKE if you got 5.

20. Just because I don't talk to you, or text you first, doesn't mean I don't miss you. I'm just waiting for you to miss me.

21. I like talking to myself, answering myself, and laughing at my own jokes.

22. I'm Not Arguing. I'm Simply Explaining Why I'm Right.

23. LIKE if you always wonder if someone, somewhere is doing the same exact thing as you are.

24. People think I'm in a bad mood just because I'm being quiet.

25. I turned my phone onto "Airplane mode" and threw it up into the air. Worst. Transformer. Ever.

Get Daily "Top" Funny Statuses @ www.FunnyStatus.com

Top 25 Status Updates 2011

1. Today I went on thesaurus.com & searched "ninjas." The computer told me, "Ninjas cannot be found." Well played, ninjas, well played.

2. That awkward moment when someone spells your name wrong on Facebook even though your name is RIGHT THERE!

3. When someone smells nice, it automatically makes them more attractive.

4. Rhinos are just fat unicorns.

5. Our generation doesn't knock on doors. We will call or text to let you know we're outside.

6. If people could read my mind, I'd get punched in the face a lot.

7. LIKE IF: You sat down to check Facebook real quick and an hour later, you're still here.

8. Don't you hate it when you have an older family member on Facebook and they comment on EVERYTHING you do?

9. The biggest mistake I have made in my life is letting people stay in my life far longer than they deserve.

10. The awkward moment when someone says something to you for the fifth time and you still don't know what they said.

11. You know a girl just broke up with her boyfriend when she starts putting a million quotes on Facebook.

12. No comments or LIKEs after 5 minutes. Delete post, hope no one saw or calls you out.

13. That awkward moment when you're supposed to be cleaning your room and you put on music and it turns into a dance party for one.

14. I am NOT single, and I am NOT taken. I'm simply on reserve for the one who REALLY deserves to have my heart.

15. I think I have a serious problem. Today I was reading the newspaper and found myself looking for the "Like" button.

16. The good thing about having a bad memory is that jokes can be funny more than once.

17. *Wake up in middle of night, look at clock* Yes! I still have time to sleep.

18. The length of your "about me" section on Facebook is directly proportional to how annoying you are in real life.

19. I hate when it's quiet and you're eating something crunchy.

20. Flies are everywhere, unfortunately the second I grab the fly swatter, they turn into ninjas.

21. Whenever I delete an App on my iPhone, the shaking icons make me feel like they're all panicked over who's getting deleted.

22. Don't feel special. I only keep your number in my phone so I know not to answer when you call.

23. I don't make typos. I make new words.

24. 3 words, 8 letters, 3 syllables, 5 vowels, 3 consonants, 2 nouns, 1 emotion, many meanings, a big lie, a rare truth: I LOVE YOU!

25. Morning Routine: 1. Wake Up 2. Check phone for messages 3. Check Facebook for any notifications.

Bonus Top Statuses for 2011...

☞ That awkward moment when you don't know if you should hold the door for someone or not.

- Perfect people aren't real, and real people aren't perfect. So you can either love people for their flaws, or hate them because they're real.
- Facebook should get an "I don't even know you" button, for the people who try to add people they don't know.
- Sometimes I read status updates on Facebook and wonder, "How am I friends with them?" Then I remember I am not actually friends with them.
- Dear iTunes, please realize that when I put you on "shuffle," I mean, "play all of my favorite songs." Sincerely, skip... skip... skip...
- Oh so now I'm invisible to you? That's cool. I've always wanted a superpower.
- That awkward moment when you post a status on Facebook and someone likes it almost immediately.
- Don't leave something good to see if you can find better, because once you realize you had the best, the best found better.
- My alarm clock is jealous of the relationship I have with my bed. It always tries to wake me up!

- My teacher is always talking to her imaginary friend named "Class."
- I'm not lazy...I'm just highly motivated to do absolutely nothing today.
- LIKE if you check your phone to see what time it is and then check it again because the first time you weren't paying attention.
- You wanna know who's amazing & has the cutest smile ever? Read the first word again :)

Top Status Updates Of Previous Years...

2010

1. "Are you as bored as I am?" Read that backwards, it still makes sense.
2. Unwritten Facebook rule #5: If that person isn't in the photo, don't tag them.
3. Your life is a book; don't jump to the end to see if it's worth it. Just enjoy life and fill those pages with beautiful memories.

4. Going to: ☐ Paris ☐ New York ☐ London ✔ KITCHEN, I'm hungry.

5. That awkward moment when you have 10 tabs open and you cant figure out which one the music is coming from.

6. Just realized: "Google before you status update" is the new "think before you speak."

7. LIKE IF you... walk into a room, forget what you need, walk out, and then remember.

8. When someone says the words "I love you" and you don't feel the same way, just say "I love YOUTUBE" real fast.

9. Kidnapping is such a strong word. I prefer to think of it as Surprise Adoption.

10. When I say I want someone with a sense of humor I mean I want someone with MY sense of humor.

2009

1. The fact that music can induce goose bumps, draw a tear, inspire, and connect is one of my favorite parts of being a human.

2. That annoying person who always tries to destroy your logic on your Facebook statuses because they think they're smarter than you.

3. I looked up "thesaurus" in my thesaurus and it says, "Don't be a smart-ass."

4. ♥ Love me now ♥ Love me never ♥ But if You Love Me ♥ Love me Forever ♥

5. Thanks to Facebook, I now know what everyone's bathroom looks like 1 mirror at a time.

6. 1. You Get Robbed. 2. Update Facebook Status. 3. Tweet About It. 4. Call 911.

7. That awkward moment when you have to explain a dirty joke to someone.

8. Why can't they make the whole week out of Saturdays?

9. I believe in sharing the road with other drivers. They can have the part behind me.

10. There are two rules to success in life: 1. Don't tell people everything you know.

2008

1. Does anyone really "Laugh Out Loud" when they write LOL?

2. I just bought a blindfold, can't see myself wearing it though.

3. A boy gave a girl 13 roses, 12 were real, one was fake, then the boy said to the girl, I will love you till the last rose dies.

4. I just sprayed a mosquito with mosquito repellant. Now, he'll never have any friends.

5. Talking louder does not make you any less wrong.

6. Don't underestimate the power of stupid people in large numbers.

7. People who gossip with you, most likely gossip about you.

8. If your plan A doesn't work, don't sweat it. The alphabet has 25 more letters.

9. If you have a problem face it, don't Facebook it!

10. I turn down my radio to park my car.

TOP 10 WORST STATUS UPDATES

It's awful to have to sort through irrelevant, unfunny, attention-spawning status updates just to get to the good stuff like who's dating who, and the plastic surgery that went crazy-wrong.

Not that you are guilty of it (wink, wink), but many Facebookers are at fault for chocking up the worst status updates of all time. In order of annoyance:

1. "Can't read my, can't read my, no he can't read my Poker face..."

Honestly? Is that even necessary, Ms. Pop Princess? We all have those friends – you know the ones – the music specialists? The pop kings and queens? Perhaps even the rap emcees out there who think it's an act of genius to post music as their status. It's tough to imagine someone typing up a song lyric as their status update, posting it, and thinking it's cool.

2. The Passive Aggressor

Isn't it fun seeing someone take their psychological dismay out on Facebook? The passive-aggressive types think it's a great idea to post a little dig on Facebook. What's funny is they actually think the object of that aggression is going to read it. Nope.

3. TMI – Too Much Information

Oh yes, the status updates about one's gynecological problems, financial troubles, husband's baby mama drama, bad debts, and the like are probably TMI even for your closest friends. No really, it's true. And plus, how many Facebookers actually keep their list to close friends only? Do you really want your co-worker, Debbie, knowing about your "irregular bowel movements"?

4. Too Cool for School

You may be a whiz at ColdFusion, but most of your friends probably aren't, so posting your amazing C++ creation isn't going to jive with your friends. You may look cool to your technical friends, but the rest of them are probably chuckling at your expense. Save the fun techy lingo for a night out with the geeks!

5. The One Uppers

Okay, so you scored a date with James Franco, need to buy new jeans because your size 0s are "too loose," ate at newest restaurant downtown (that has reservations 3 months out), and hired a personal sushi chef. Whoopee.

6. The Annoying Teaser

Posting something ambiguous like, "Guess what just happened?" is kind of like asking which hand the rubber ball is in behind your back. A little childish, a little fun – but still annoying on the side of desperate. Oops, yeah, we said it!

7. One Word Update

Tired. Hungry. Bored. Yeah. We. Get it…yawn.

8. The...

So, wait, are you asking, telling, and saying – what's really going on here? Was there a typo? Don't get it. So wait, what?

9. Mr. Marketer

"Hey! Check out this cool website!" is a common Facebook standard. We see it all the time. That's cool if you're just Joe Schmo posting to John Doe's wall, but the constant marketing from certain companies is a buzz-kill. Don't choke the golden goose.

10. Story Status Updates

All right, these are exhausting. It's the friend who just purchased her new computer. But wait, now the manual is missing. Okay! Neat, found the manual! Just powered it up, wondering how to upload new software? Just uploaded new software, yay for Microsoft Word! Hey, does anyone know where to find the product registration key? Honestly – no one cares.

Bonus Annoying Status Updates:

We would like to add the following notes about your annoying Facebook updates:

1. We don't want to hear about your new pet puppy. Good luck with him crapping all over the place.
2. Sucks you two broke up - keep it to yourself and get over it already.
3. Congrats on your vacation but there is no need to rub it in my face that everyone isn't in Hawaii.

ENHANCING FACEBOOK WITH APPS

Everybody is talking about apps! Facebook provides a platform for developers to create hugely popular applications. Apps can be used in limitless ways to enhance your Facebook experience making it easier for you and also more rewarding. People also love to talk about apps!

Fact: In 2009 Farmville was the #1 term mentioned in status updates.

Although games are a blast on Facebook, there are also tons of useful utility apps that will simplify your Facebook experience.

For example, we provide a free "Funny Status" Facebook app:

https://apps.facebook.com/funny-status-updates/

This allows you to pick from thousands of our best status updates from various topics in an easy to understand format.

Let's take a look at some of the most important Facebook apps to make for a rich experience:

1. **Mobile Apps:** You access Facebook the majority of time from your mobile device anyway. It's important to find quality Facebook related apps that can interact directly from your phone or tablet.

   Go to:

   http://App.net/Funny

   to download the Mobile App for iPhone, Android, and other platforms and get thousands of daily updated funny statuses direct to your phone along with tons of other great features!

Other Social Networking Mobile Apps worth checking out: Instagram, Foursquare, Path, Pinterest, Quora, HootSuite, Twitter

2. **Facebook Apps:** Lets face it, it's tough to wade through the thousands of pointless apps on Facebook and get to the ones that are actually awesome. Here are our recommendations to enhance your time on Facebook...

Spotify *(www.facebook.com/Spotify)*

Listen to free music with your friends and enhance your Timeline with this amazingly simple app.

Pinterest *(www.facebook.com/pinterest)*

Discover cool new things and PIN things you find while browsing the internet. This addictive app will leave you wondering what happened to all of your time?

FoodSpotting *(www.facebook.com/Foodspotting)*

Really neat way to experience restaurants by the dishes they serve and not the "general type of food" classification. If you're a Foodie, this app is a must!

Vevo *(www.facebook.com/VEVO)*

Make your Timeline ROCK with this music video slinging application.

Goodreads *(www.facebook.com/Goodreads)*

This is a fabulous way to share everything book related. What you're reading (HINT: THIS BOOK!), what you're friends are reading, what you want to read, etc.

Turntable *(http://turntable.fm/)*

Ever wanted to play DJ??? Now you can play LIVE DJ with all of your Facebook friends without having them over and wrecking your house with this neat app!

Fab *(www.facebook.com/fab.com)*

A must-have for any shopaholic out there. This app makes social sharing of your favorite purchases as simple as pie.

TripAdvisor *(www.tripadvisor.com/)*

Everyone loves to share their travels on Facebook. Well, it just got simpler with this Timeline integrated app that makes planning and sharing your trips 10x easier.

The Onion *(www.theonion.com/)*

We hate to admit when we find a website that's funnier than ours but, The Onion is hysterical. The dry satire will leave you laughing for days and this app will have your friends both confused and crying with laughter after they realize the link they just clicked isn't a real news story.

FanDango *(www.fandango.com/)*

Share your popcorn diary about the latest blockbuster you just saw with this app.

PART 2

CATEGORIZED STATUS UPDATES

ANIMAL STATUS UPDATES

- You've cat to be kitten me right meow.
- I love Pandas, they're so chill. They're like "Dude, racism is stupid. I'm White, Black, and Asian."
- The reason dogs scratch themselves is because no one else knows where they itch.
- This is like 7 dog status updates.
- Oh a spider. You are tiny. I am a great big person. I am a grown up. I can handle this. You are tiny. I am a great big pers- OMG IT MOVED!!

- ☞ I wonder if sharks have a Human Week.
- ☞ OMG! I can levitate birds!
- ☞ Everyone has pretended to die in front their pets to see if they would do anything.
- ☞ A dog made out of diamonds is everyone's best friend.
- ☞ Why do they try to make pet food in TV commercials look good to humans?
- ☞ My relationship with my cat is like that of a married couple. Basically we fight a lot and never have sex.
- ☞ Laughing stock: cattle with a sense of humor.
- ☞ When someone rings the doorbell, why do dogs always assume it's for them?
- ☞ Thinks that wishing your pets could talk is fun until you remember everything you've ever done in front of your pets.
- ☞ Why is there a show called "When Animals Attack"? It should be called "When Stupid People Go Near Dangerous Animals." That would be a more appropriate name.
- ☞ Dogs have masters. Cats have staff.

- ☞ Life is like a bird, it's pretty cute until it craps on you.
- ☞ Hippopotomonstrosesquippedaliophobia: Fear of long words.
- ☞ If a turtle doesn't have a shell, is he homeless or naked?
- ☞ The winner of the rat race is still a rat.
- ☞ Did you know that dolphins are so smart that within a few weeks of captivity, they can train people to stand on the very edge of the pool and throw them fish?
- ☞ When I die, I want to be buried with some random animal bone like a giraffe ... just to confuse future archaeologists.

THE AWKWARD MOMENT WHEN...

- ☞ You've already said "what?" three times and still have no idea what the person said, so you just agree.
- ☞ You can't stop laughing while telling a joke and when you're finally done your friends don't even get it.
- ☞ Sarcasm doesn't work in a text.
- ☞ Someone's zipper is down and you don't know whether to tell, because you can't explain why you were looking that low.
- ☞ You check the price tag, and sadly, go away.

- ☞ You're late for class, and when you walk in, everyone stares at you like you killed someone.
- ☞ A sentence doesn't end the way you think it octopus.
- ☞ You get tagged in a photo on a night, at a place that you said you weren't.
- ☞ Your Facebook status gets no "likes."
- ☞ The person you like is online and you just open the chat window but don't know what to say.
- ☞ You suddenly remember something really hilarious in a silent situation.
- ☞ There's an awkward moment, and everyone knows it's an awkward moment, then somebody says, "AWWWKKKKWAAARRDD!"
- ☞ Someone catches you staring at them.
- ☞ Your dancing, then you turn around and you realize someone has been watching you the WHOLE time.
- ☞ Someone isn't texting you back and then you see them update their status from their mobile.

- ☞ You have to make up an excuse to not hang out with someone because you'd rather chill at home.
- ☞ You're singing really loudly to a song and then someone changes it without warning.
- ☞ You understand something after the test.
- ☞ You pour your cereal into the bowl thinking you have milk...only to realize you don't have milk at all.
- ☞ You're yelling at someone and you mess up a word.
- ☞ You post a funny status on Facebook and someone has to ruin it by commenting being all serious!
- ☞ Your crush asks you, "Who do you like?"
- ☞ Your mother compares you to another kid and she has no idea how much worse they are than you.
- ☞ You say goodbye to someone and you end up walking in the same direction.
- ☞ Someone walks in on you singing to yourself.

- ☞ You think you're talking to your friend but then realize you're talking to a stranger beside you.
- ☞ You shout the wrong answer in class with confidence.
- ☞ You get into one little fight and your mum gets scared and makes you move in with your auntie and uncle in Bel-air.
- ☞ Someone brings up an embarrassing moment from your past that you do not wish to be reminded of.
- ☞ The awkward moment when halfway through telling a story you realize it is pointless.
- ☞ You realize you've been pronouncing a word wrong your whole life.
- ☞ The dentist asks you a question while their whole hand is shoved in your mouth.
- ☞ You're telling your friend something hilarious and they're just like "you already told me."
- ☞ You throw your phone because you're angry, then get freaked out that it

might be broken & wonder why you threw it.

- ☞ You see your classmate in public and you both act as though you've never seen each other before.

- ☞ Preschool kids have a more successful love life than you :/

- ☞ You attempt to tickle someone's armpit and end up feeling the moist on your fingers.

- ☞ You "LIKE" someone's status on Facebook by accident because of your touchscreen phone.

- ☞ You're sitting there in the movies and you think something is funny and you burst out laughing and nobody else is and everyone stares at you.

- ☞ You realize someone was actually home the whole time you were singing at the top of your lungs.

- ☞ A film says, "based on a true story" and it automatically becomes 100 times scarier.

- ☞ Two people start a conversation on YOUR Facebook status.

☞ You get emotionally attached to a celebrity you have never met.

☞ You have such an awesome ringtone you decide never to answer your phone again.

☞ You slam a door closed by accident. No, no guys, I'm not upset, I swear.

☞ Someone tells you how much they hate someone, and then the next day they're best friends.

☞ You go through your phone so you don't feel alone in public places.

☞ You're trying to explain how a song goes, but you really don't want to sing it.

☞ You're looking for something and it was in your hand or right in front of you the whole time.

☞ You're in the car driving, singing loud and your phone decides to call someone and they just listen...

☞ You start telling a story and you realize no one's listening, so you slowly fade out and pretend you never said anything.

- ☞ You see 9-year-olds in a relationship, while you're still single.
- ☞ Everyone is talking in class except for you.
- ☞ That awkward moment when you are ignoring a call and accidentally answer it.
- ☞ That awkward moment when you're yelling at someone and you mess up a word.

COMPUTER STATUS UPDATES

- Me without you is like Facebook WITHOUT FRIENDS, YOUTUBE WITHOUT VIDEOS and Google WITH NO RESULTS.
- I hate when websites ask, "Are you a human?" Umm hello? I'm obviously a unicorn.
- I'd get a lot more sleep if I didn't insist on reading the entire Internet every night.
- I've just started a band called 999 Megabytes. We haven't done a gig yet.
- Have you ever had a fly or small bug land on your computer screen and your first reaction is to try and scare it with the cursor?

☞ Saying bye to someone... then staying online for another 2 hours.

☞ They really need to add a "download this song illegally" button on Pandora.

☞ Sleep is so cute when it tries to compete with the Internet.

☞ The most adventurous I get is visiting Amazon on my Safari.

☞ Every time I see a field for "promotion code" during checkout all I can think is "I'm getting overcharged for this."

☞ Life is way too short to safely remove a USB.

☞ "All you do is sit on that computer." Lies. I sit on the chair.

☞ Forgetting to close my tab at the bar isn't as costly as forgetting to close tabs on my computer at home.

☞ iPhone + iMac + iPod + iPad = iBroke

☞ The people who invented the Internet never would have got around to doing it if they had the Internet.

☞ Sometimes life just needs a good, hard CTRL ALT DELETE.

☞ Save as: fjhdsk ... The file fjhdsk already exists ... fjhdsk 2.

- ☞ My Internet is so slow, it would be faster to just drive to Google's headquarters and ask them this in person.
- ☞ Where do all the characters go that you type on the keyboard before you realize the cursor isn't in the box?
- ☞ Life before the computer: Memory was something that you lost with age. An application was for employment. A program was a TV show. A cursor used profanity. A keyboard was a piano. A web was a spider's home. A virus was the flu. A CD was a bank account. A hard drive was a long trip on the road. A mouse pad was where a mouse lived. And if you had a 3 1/2 inch floppy...you just hoped nobody found out.
- ☞ Is it just me or does anyone else occasionally have to look up a word while they are writing, that they have known how to spell for most of their life, because it just doesn't look quite right?
- ☞ Sometimes I wish the "Reply All" button was password protected.
- ☞ Every time I pull a flash drive out of a computer I feel like a spy.

CUTE STATUS UPDATES

- ☞ If anyone catches me singing in my car, my immediate reaction is to stare at them until it is equally awkward for both of us.
- ☞ I'm crazy. I'm funny. I'm cute. I'm brave. I'm girly. I'm sweet. I'm cheerful. I'm annoying. I'm just me & I like it like that!
- ☞ "Let's settle this the mature adult way." "Rock paper scissors?" "Yep..."
- ☞ I'm actually not funny. I'm just really mean & people think I'm joking.

- I'm the type of person who laughs at a joke 3 times: when it's told, when it's explained & 5 minutes later when I finally get it.
- LIKE IF you randomly talk "ghetto" with your best-friend ;)
- If you never jumped from couch to couch as kid to avoid the lava, then you missed out on childhood.
- Let your past make you better not bitter.
- The attractive face you pull just before a sneeze.
- When someone appears in your dreams, it means that person misses you.
- Hey, what's up? Oh wait... it's just the ceiling.
- The worst things in life are also free.
- There's always a little truth behind every "just kidding," a little reason behind every "just wondering," a little knowledge behind every "I don't know," and a little feeling behind every "I don't care."

- ☞ I love it when the person's laugh is funnier than the actual joke.
- ☞ When you're right, no one remembers. When you're wrong, no one forgets.
- ☞ When life gives you a hundred reasons to cry, show life that you have a thousand reasons to smile.
- ☞ I'm old enough to know what's bad for me and young enough to do it.
- ☞ Everyone has that one friend you just can't bring anywhere cause they always embarrass you. If you can't think of who that friend is, it's you.
- ☞ Someone said you look like an owl. WHO??? WHOOOOO????

FACEBOOK STATUS UPDATES

- Life is like Facebook. People will LIKE your problems & comment, but no one will solve them because everyone is busy updating theirs.

- The "people you may know" feature on FB should be renamed to "people that you know, but deliberately choose not to be friends with."

- What Is FACEBOOK?...It's a place where a Guy posts a joke, he gets No Response... and if a Girl posts the same Joke, She gets 150 Likes, 300 Comments & 60 Friends Requests.

- ☞ Facebook = Heavily populated city. Twitter = Just a vacation spot. Myspace = A ghost town.
- ☞ Dear Facebook, I can't believe you still haven't gotten that dislike button. Sincerely, YouTube.
- ☞ Sitting on Facebook liking random stuff because you're bored.
- ☞ Facebook needs the following 3 buttons: "Dislike," "Who cares?" and "Are you stupid?"
- ☞ Some people should get two Facebook accounts... one for each face.
- ☞ A person liking my status from a week ago on Facebook proves that I have stalkers.
- ☞ The day Facebook adds an option that you can like that someone liked something, I quit the Internet forever.
- ☞ If "real life" were really that great, Facebook wouldn't be so darn addictive.
- ☞ FACEBOOK: The second most popular word that starts with "F" and ends with "K."

- ☞ IMAGINE if Facebook, Twitter, and msn all broke at the same time. We might have to actually get lives.

- ☞ Fridge full of food - Nothing to eat. Wardrobe full of clothes - Nothing to wear. Internet full of sites - only on Facebook.

- ☞ At least clean up the bathroom before taking your profile picture in there.

- ☞ It's only but so long you can hide behind a good profile pic... random photo tags will expose you!

- ☞ When I die, I'd like someone to keep updating my Facebook status just to freak people out... "Hey, who knew they had Wi-Fi up here?"

- ☞ There are three kinds of lies... Lies, Damned Lies and Status Updates.

- ☞ Facebook is a great excuse to talk to your self without looking stupid :)

- ☞ My greatest fear is that I will accidentally use the status update as the search bar.

- ☞ Facebook: a place where people announce their problems to the world but not to the person they have a problem with.

☞ Facebook should change the status question from "What's on your mind?" to "What's your problem today?"

☞ Didn't Comment or LIKE my picture huh? NOTED!

☞ Facebook. The brain laxative.

☞ I'm texting random phone numbers with "I just saw your Facebook Status. LOL"!

☞ Reading someone's status and thinking "OH CRY ME A RIVER"

☞ You know you've done a great job when somebody you DON'T know LIKEs your status.

☞ To Do List... 1. Make to do list ✓ 2. Check off first thing on to do list ✓ 3. Realize you've already accomplished 2 things ✓ 4. Reward yourself with nap (in progress)

☞ If you want to cry use a tissue; not your Facebook status.

☞ Facebook: ... -Log on -Check notifications -Poke everyone back -Go on homepage

-Do the happy birthday ritual -Go back to homepage -Change from Top news to Most recent -Have a little scroll down -Like a couple of pages –You're bored already.

- ☞ Cheated on Facebook with my real life today.

- ☞ Top reasons to like a status: 1. Hahaha. That's pretty funny. 2. I completely agree. 3. I know that this is about me, so I'm purposefully liking it. 4. I like you.

- ☞ Do you ever think of a clever Facebook status, but you had already posted one for that day so you had to wait?

- ☞ I SAW YOUR COMMENT BEFORE YOU DELETED IT.

- ☞ PROFILE PICTURES: What people want other people to think they look like. TAGGED PICTURES: What they actually look like.

FAMILY STATUS UPDATES

- ☞ If my mom can't find it, nobody can find it.
- ☞ "Dad I'm hungry." "Nice to meet you hungry!" "Dad, I'm serious..." "I thought you were hungry?" "Are you kidding?!" "No, I'm Dad."
- ☞ You can't choose your family.... but you can ignore their phone calls.
- ☞ I believe that every person has a story to tell...which is why I stay home.
- ☞ "I need to talk to you" is the one sentence that has the power to make

you remember every bad thing you've ever done in your life.

- "Clean your room, Family are coming over" ... "Oh, I'm sorry, I didn't realize the gathering would be held in my bedroom."
- Everything magically appears when your mom looks for it...
- The fake laugh you do when an old person cracks a joke.
- Stupidity runs in the family... It's a good thing I'm adopted.
- All mothers have intuition. Great mothers have radar.
- My mother said, "You won't amount to anything because you procrastinate." I said, "Oh ya...Just you wait."
- If friends could be bought at the store, I'd buy you. And I'd get a good deal because those "slightly irregular" bins are always discounted.
- Happiness is having a large, loving, caring, close-knit family... in another city.
- Home is where you can say anything you like 'cause nobody listens to you anyway.

FOOD STATUS UPDATES

- ☞ I'm not hungry. But, I am bored. Therefore, I shall eat... :D
- ☞ Am I the only one who opens a loaf of bread and skips the first slice because it's ugly?
- ☞ I put the "toast" in "toaster." Then I take the "toast" out of the "toaster."
- ☞ Cheese is like a villain from a horror movie: Whatever you do to it only makes it stronger. Shred it? Better. Slice it? Better. Melt it? Perfection.

- *Food hits ground* Germ: "GET IT!!!" King germ: "No, you have to wait at least 5 seconds!"

- Vegetarians...if you love animals so much, why do you keep eating all of their food?

- A seafood diet is the best: whenever you see food, eat it.

- It's time to clean the refrigerator when something closes the door from the inside.

- Anything Fried + Ranch = Win

- Chickens: The only animal you eat before they are born and after they are dead.

- Hey Potato Chips, you forgot to list "air" under the ingredients... thanks for nothing!

- BACON (Noun)- 1. A type of meat derived from pig. 2. The main reason I'm not a vegetarian.

- If tomatoes are classed as a fruit, then doesn't that mean that ketchup is technically a smoothie?

- ☞ If they ever put a DUI checkpoint at a Taco Bell drive-thru, it's safe to say we're all screwed.
- ☞ Big deal, McDonalds. We're all here for a limited time only.
- ☞ Knowledge is knowing a tomato is a fruit. Wisdom is not putting it in a fruit salad.
- ☞ Grocery store aisles should have a fast lane.
- ☞ If we are what we eat, I'm fast, cheap and easy.
- ☞ BEST INVENTION EVER: Being able to download food from the Internet.
- ☞ I hate it when you drink water and the ice attacks your face.
- ☞ Screw you recommended serving size. You don't know me.
- ☞ Drink coffee! Do stupid things faster with more energy!
- ☞ Sometimes it's just easier to eat the last slice of pizza than fit the box in the fridge.
- ☞ The four food groups: Fast, Frozen, Instant, and Chocolate.

- ☞ I only want two things in life:
  1. Lose weight
  2. Eat.

- ☞ When I was a kid, I used to close the fridge door slowly just to see when the light turned off.

FUNNY QUESTIONS

- If the sky's the limit, then what is space? Over the limit?
- Why do some movie previews feel the need to show you almost the entire movie?
- Why are you always the only one in your house that knows how to put a new toilet paper roll on the holder?
- Did you ever notice the people who say money isn't everything are usually really rich?
- Who else speaks sarcasm as a second language?

- Why is it when you transport something by car it's called a shipment but when you transport by ship it's called cargo?
- Do you ever wonder why W is called Double U, when it's clearly Double V?
- Don't you hate when the person you're Facebook-stalking never updates anything?
- If all the nations in the world are in debt, who's got all the money?
- How come you never read about a psychic winning the lottery?
- Doesn't expecting the unexpected make the unexpected become the expected?
- Do fish get thirsty?
- Why is bra singular and panties plural?
- Why is Greenland made of ice and Iceland made of green grass?
- Why do people always say "no offense" right before they offend you?
- Why do people who sing the loudest tend to be the ones who are the most off key?

- ☞ How come when socks come out of the dryer, there's only one of each?
- ☞ Why does some moist towelette packages come with instructions that read, "Open package and use" - what else would you do with them?
- ☞ Why do some products state, "Not recommended for children over 12 years of age" - aren't people over 12 years of age not children?
- ☞ Why is the man who handles all your money called a broker?
- ☞ Does anyone ever vanish with a trace?
- ☞ Why do they call the airport a terminal if flying is supposed to be safe?
- ☞ How come people never get talker's block?
- ☞ If you drop hand sanitizer on the floor, does it clean the floor or does the floor get it dirty?
- ☞ Why do restaurants offer appetizers - don't you already have an appetite if you're there?

- ☞ What color is a chameleon on a plaid shirt?
- ☞ If steroids are illegal for athletes, shouldn't Photoshop be illegal models?
- ☞ What do you call a male ladybug?
- ☞ If nobody's perfect... Does that make us Nobody?
- ☞ If we threw you a going away party, would you?

HEALTH STATUS UPDATES

- I found a dollar in my bed this morning. Following my excitement was a flash of panic when I checked all my teeth.
- "Why are kids obese? Maybe because Burgers are $.99, & Salads are $4.99."
- Cool little fact... You can't hum if you plug your nose... bet you've just tried it. LOL
- My brain hurts. That means it's getting stronger. Right?
- Yawning is your body's way of saying 20% of battery remaining.

- I honestly don't care if you think I'm crazy. You're just a figment of my imagination anyway.
- I have lots of great personality traits. Or as my doctor calls them, symptoms.
- I would never go bungee jumping. A broken rubber brought me into this world, and it's not going to take me out.
- CHILL OUT. This is gym, not the Olympics.
- Don't think of it as getting a flu shot. Think of it as installing virus protection software.
- Life is like a mirror; we get the best results when we smile at it.
- Health plans are like hospital gowns... you only think you're covered.
- Increasingly, I'm feeling like a used car. My body's shot, my rear end's dragging and I can't keep my hood up.
- I just signed up for a well-known diet plan. So far, all I've lost is $200.
- Why do they use sterilized needles for death by lethal injection?

- ☞ People on TV always give such accurate descriptions of criminals to sketch artists. I look at myself every chance I get and I don't think I could get my own face right.
- ☞ Forget the health food. I need all the preservatives I can get.
- ☞ If 4 out of 5 people SUFFER from diarrhea... does that mean that one enjoys it?
- ☞ I don't suffer from insanity. I enjoy every minute of it.
- ☞ They say, "You are what you eat" so I guess we should eat skinny people.
- ☞ I have to exercise early in the morning before my brain figures out what I'm doing.
- ☞ Cigarettes are like hamsters. They are completely harmless until you put them in your mouth and set them on fire.
- ☞ I didn't fight my way to the top of the food chain to be a vegetarian.
- ☞ My psychiatrist told me I was crazy and I said I want a second opinion. He said okay, you're ugly too.

- WARNING: The consumption of alcohol may cause you to think you can sing.
- I may be fat, but you're ugly - I can lose weight!
- My brain is giving me the silent treatment.
- I wonder if butterflies get humans in their stomach when they're anxious?
- I just coughed and sneezed at the same time, I think I traveled 3 seconds into the future.
- I would be much thinner if I hadn't gained all this weight.
- Good health is merely the slowest possible rate at which one can die.

KID STATUS UPDATES

- ☞ 8-year-olds today have Facebook, Twitter, phones, iPods. When I was their age, I had a coloring book, crayons, chalk, and imagination.

- ☞ A friend would share a bag of chips, but a best-friend would eat them all then give you the empty bag and say "You can have the rest."

- ☞ Today I saw a baby with a bib that said "This dumbass put my cape on backwards."

- ☞ I hate when your mad at someone and they make you laugh.

- ☞ Your mom decides to be in the room while you're on the computer, so you just switch to Google and stare at it.

- ☞ Children: You spend the first 2 years of their life teaching them to walk and talk. Then you spend the next 16 years telling them to sit down and shut-up.

- ☞ I totally take back all those times I didn't want to nap when I was younger.

- ☞ When I have kids I'm gonna tell them drugs are good for them. It's the only way I can be sure they won't try them.

- ☞ Do you remember when you were a kid, playing Nintendo and it wouldn't work? You take the cartridge out, blow in it and that would magically fix the problem. Every kid in America did that, but how did we all know how to fix the problem? There was no Internet or message boards or F.A.Q.'s. We just figured it out. Today's kids are soft.

- ☞ I love asking little kids what they want to be when they grow up, cause, you know, I'm still looking for ideas.

- ☞ If you want your children to listen to you, try talking softly to someone else.

- ☞ You know your children are growing up when they stop asking you where they came from and refuse to tell you where they're going.

- ☞ When I was a kid I had to blow into my video games to get them to work.

- ☞ A true friend will never get in your way ... unless you are on your way down.

- ☞ Your kid may be an honors student, but you're still an idiot.

- ☞ Kids shouldn't be sad. Ever. That's what your adult life is for.

- ☞ Parent, because I said so. Child, Whatever. Grandma, Bingo!

- ☞ Cleaning your house while your kids are still growing is like shoveling the driveway before it has stopped snowing.

- ☞ I want kids. I have chores to assign.

- ☞ A child's greatest period of growth is the month after you've purchased new school clothes.

- ☞ 9 out of 10 kids named Jeeves probably grow up to be butlers.

- I wish it were socially acceptable to wear sweatpants all the time.
- Insanity is hereditary. You get it from your kids.
- Kids are like little drunk people.
- The new parent threat: "Stop doing that or I will take a picture and put it on Facebook for the world to see."

LIFE STATUS UPDATES

- I just read a list of "100 things to do before you die." And, I've got to say that I'm pretty surprised "yell for help" wasn't one of them.
- I'm Not Arguing. I'm Simply Explaining Why I'm Right.
- I like talking to myself, answering myself, and laughing at my own jokes.
- If people could read my mind, I'd get punched in the face a lot.
- Remember when phones were stupid and people were smart? Ahh Good times.

- I'm not lazy...I'm just highly motivated to do absolutely nothing today.
- It doesn't matter what other people think about you. The only thing that matters is that you are happy with who you are.
- Your life is a book; don't jump to the end to see if it's worth it. Just enjoy life and fill those pages with beautiful memories.
- The past is history, the future is a mystery, today is a gift...that's why they call it the "present"!
- Old meaning of sorry. "I won't do it again." New meaning of sorry. "Damn I got caught, next time I need to be more careful."
- I ignore texts. I let the phone ring. It's nothing personal, but some people need to realize that sometimes I don't feel like talking.
- I was going to do something, but I got distracted for 5 seconds and now I forgot what I was doing.

- ☞ Funny how when you're not looking sometimes life can show you a better view.
- ☞ You have one advantage over me, you can kiss my ass and I can't.
- ☞ Most of the time when people judge you, they have more problems than you do.
- ☞ In life, you have two choices: get over it or die with it on your mind.
- ☞ Throughout life: I've loved, I've lied, I've hurt, I've lost, I've missed, I've trusted, I've made mistakes, but most of all, I've learned.
- ☞ My life. My choices. My mistakes. My lessons. Not your business.
- ☞ When I say "wow, that's crazy," 99% of the time, it means I haven't been listening to a word of your conversation.
- ☞ Memories make us who we are. Dreams make us who we will become.
- ☞ Has learned that you can't please everyone... but you can piss them all off at the same time!

☞ Before you talk, listen. Before you react, think. Before you criticize, wait. Before you pray, forgive. Before you quit, try.

☞ I wish I could autocorrect my life.

☞ Surround yourself with people who make you laugh and smile so that you can forget the bad and focus solely on the good.

☞ Life is not fair, but life is not fair for everyone... which actually makes it fair.

☞ Be yourself—everyone else is already taken.

☞ This is how my week goes:
Mooooooooooooonday
Tuuuuuuuuuuuuesday
Weeeeeeeeeeednesday
Thuuuuuuuuuuursday
FridaySaturdaySunday.

☞ My daily needs: Food-5%, Water-1%, Sleep-4%, Internet-90%.

☞ Laughter is a smile with the volume turned up.

☞ The road to success is always under construction.

- Life is full of lessons that were taught on the day that I missed class.
- I could do great things if I weren't so busy doing little things.
- People will believe anything if you whisper it.
- LIFE WOULD BE BETTER IF some girls had mute buttons, guys had edit buttons, bad times had fast forward buttons & good times had pause buttons.
- Don't hang around people who have given up on their dreams because they are coming after yours next.
- The past cannot be changed, forgotten, edited or erased. It can only be accepted.
- It's been a lifetime struggle for me to stop spending my lifetime struggling.
- People say that things happen for a reason. So when I hit you up side the head, remember I had a reason.
- Society needs both optimists and pessimists. For example, an optimist invented the airplane while a pessimist invented the parachute.

- ☞ Don't make decisions when you're angry. Don't make promises when you're happy.
- ☞ Never explain yourself. Your friends don't need it and your enemies won't believe it.
- ☞ Deaf to bullshit, blind to fake shit. Stop wasting your time on people who don't deserve to be an issue in your life.
- ☞ After a Hurricane, comes a Rainbow (:
- ☞ If it weren't for law enforcement and physics, I'd be unstoppable!
- ☞ Never be afraid to take a chance. You're going to die, might as well be while doing something interesting.
- ☞ People get too caught up in what others think. Just have fun with life and do what makes you happy.
- ☞ If you don't like my sense of humor please tell me... so I can laugh at you!
- ☞ That terrifying moment when you rub your eyes for too long and you go blind for like 10 seconds.

- ☞ I don't understand you. You don't understand me. What else do we have in common?

- ☞ It isn't that I'm not a people person. It's just that I'm not a stupid people person.

- ☞ Even at your best some people won't appreciate you! But that's their problem not yours!

- ☞ Think about what you want to accomplish today and remember: All it takes - is all you've got.

- ☞ If nobody knows the troubles you've seen, then you don't live in a small town.

- ☞ We spent our whole youth to obtain wealth and our whole wealth to obtain youth.

- ☞ Life is like riding a bicycle, to keep yourself balanced you have to keep moving.

- ☞ I hate that little line of dirt that I can never get into the dustpan!

- ☞ Hope is wishing something would happen. Faith is believing something will happen. Courage is making something happen.

- The world is round, so it has no point.
- I'm so tired of people needing a reason for doing everything. Do it because you want to. Because it's fun. Because it makes you happy.
- Love, compassion and concern for others are real sources of happiness.
- Sunny today with a slight chance of me going outside to enjoy it.
- Part of being sane is being a little bit crazy.
- Normal is just a setting on your dryer.
- It is incredible how much effort I put into my laziness.
- "If you snooze you lose" is totally false. I hit the snooze button 5 times every morning and wake up feeling amazing.
- I'm not lazy, I'm energy efficient.
- They say money can't buy happiness... but it can buy bacon, and that is pretty darn close.

☞ I think you should have to pass a test to vote. Not even a complicated one, just be able to name the current president, the previous president and I don't know, the capital of your state. This would rule out at least 30% of the voters. At least.

☞ Promises are a bit like babies. Fun to make but hard to deliver.

☞ Bad decisions aren't bad if they make for good stories the next day.

☞ You don't always win your battles, but at least you fought.

☞ Remember, irresponsibility always leads to better stories.

☞ Yes, I've made mistakes… life doesn't come with instructions.

☞ If it's free, it's advice; if you pay for it, it's counseling; if you can use either one, it's a miracle!

☞ The only knowledge that can hurt you is the knowledge you don't have.

☞ Life is full of surprises. Don't believe me? Just say "never" and wait.

- ☞ He who does not understand your silence will probably not understand your words.
- ☞ Age is something that doesn't matter, unless you are a cheese.
- ☞ We make a living by what we get, we make a life by what we give.
- ☞ There are 470 tiles on my church's ceiling.
- ☞ The divorce rate among my socks is astonishing.
- ☞ It appears someone invited a lot of old people to my high school reunion.
- ☞ Life's like a bird, it's pretty cute until it dumps on your head.
- ☞ The nail that sticks out gets hammered down.
- ☞ Grades don't measure intelligence and age doesn't define maturity.
- ☞ Warning: Dates in calendar are closer than they appear.
- ☞ Am I the only one that always puts my wallet back into my pocket before getting my change back?

- ☞ Some people are wise, and some, otherwise.
- ☞ Let's pretend to get together soon.
- ☞ Haters will broadcast your failure, but whisper your success.
- ☞ Greatest fear in life... Someone will find a way to retrieve everything I've ever Googled.
- ☞ Never expect things to happen, because it's better to feel surprised than to feel disappointed.
- ☞ Life is a puzzle. You shouldn't try to place things where they're not meant to fit.
- ☞ Holding a grudge is letting someone live rent-free in your head.

LIKE IF STATUS UPDATES

- You've ever laughed so hard, no noise comes out, so you sit there clapping like a dumbfounded seal.
- You hate when you say something funny & then someone says it louder & gets the credit.
- You hate when someone tags you in a horrible picture.
- You do this: Wake up and check your Facebook like its the morning paper.
- Your texting speed automatically increases when you're angry.

- ☞ You wish you could record your dreams.
- ☞ You reply LMFAO, ROFL, or LOL and you're clearly just sitting there emotionless as a robot.
- ☞ You get a text then wait a few minutes to respond so you don't seem desperate.
- ☞ You sign on to Facebook chat & have instantly signed off upon noticing someone online.
- ☞ You've used the phrase, "Get off the phone, I have to use the Internet."
- ☞ You like food more than people.
- ☞ You hide your favorite food from your family.
- ☞ You agree with someone so they'll shut up.
- ☞ You have a mini heart attack when someone says, "Guess what I heard about you..."
- ☞ You agree...being outside counts as exercise.
- ☞ You've claimed a headache to get out of things because you're too lazy to go.
- ☞ Your parents ask you to do something and you tell them you'll do it in ten minutes then you never do it.

- ☞ You always wonder if someone, somewhere is doing the same exact thing as you are.
- ☞ You type a long paragraph with your true feelings but then erase it & type, "Yeah."
- ☞ You have that one friend that laughs at everything. Even when it's not funny.
- ☞ You HATE running out of hot water in the middle of a shower.
- ☞ You've tried to have a diary but failed epically.
- ☞ You remember growing up in the 90s and going to the Scholastic Book Fair.
- ☞ You post a status or picture, then realize you forgot something, go to delete it and someone has liked it already, putting you in an awkward position.
- ☞ You remember going to someone's MySpace page and a horrible song would start playing.
- ☞ You hate when you're listening to music really loud and you have to keep pausing it because you constantly think you're hearing your name being called.

- The last thing you do every night and the first thing you do every morning is check your phone.
- You text someone a paragraph and then 30 minutes later you get a lame reply saying LOL.
- You do this: *Ignore phone call* -Text back - "You called?"
- You delete all your texts before you give your phone to someone else.
- You read someone's text messages and can hear exactly how they would say it.
- You hate texting people first.
- You act like you're interested in the teacher's personal life just to waste time in class.
- You know someone who needs a smack in the face with a shovel.
- You shout at video games when you die.
- LIKE if...You call Gatorade by the color instead of the flavor.
- LIKE if you remember having to REWIND a video before you returned it.

LOVE STATUS UPDATES

- ☞ Dear Heart, Please stop getting involved in everything. Your job is to pump blood, that's it.

- ☞ Never chase love, affection, or attention. If another person doesn't give it freely, it isn't worth having.

- ☞ Being single doesn't mean you know nothing about love. Sometimes, it's wiser to be alone than to be with the wrong person.

- ☞ I'm a girl who usually laughs at her mistakes, so excuse me if I laugh in your face.

- I don't want to be your whole life, just your favorite part.

- If two past lovers can remain friends, either they were never in love, or they still are.

- Some say long distance relationships never succeed. I say with enough effort, time and commitment, love will find its way.

- Don't break anyone's heart; they only have one. Break they're bones. They have over 200 of them.

- It's funny how once they see that you're doing better without someone, they decide that they want you back.

- I'd rather argue with you than be with somebody else.

- Girls fall in love with what they hear; boys fall in love with what they see. That's why girls wear makeup, and boys lie.

- Admit it. You get a small rush of happiness when your crush likes your Facebook picture or status.

- ☞ I love it when I hear lyrics that totally apply to my current situation.
- ☞ It's funny how a person can break your heart, and you can still love them with all the little pieces.
- ☞ When you are in love you can't fall asleep because reality is finally better than your dreams.
- ☞ It was hard for me to walk away, but even harder when you didn't even bother to try and stop me.
- ☞ True love doesn't have a happy ending. It has NO ending.
- ☞ 3 things about REAL LOVE: 1. It doesn't hurt. 2. It doesn't leave. 3. It can never be fully explained!
- ☞ My first name and your last name sounds great together.
- ☞ They say love isn't a game. Why are there so many players then?
- ☞ Why give second chances when there are people waiting for their first?

- Love can't be proven with poems, promises, or presents. Sometimes, only pain and patience can prove it.
- I'm lucky for having you but I must say, you're luckier for having me.
- They say you don't know what you got till it's gone.... but you don't know what you've been missing, until it's arrived!
- Here's a random idea, just out of the blue. How about you fall for me, as hard as I fell for you?
- Deleting my feelings for you. ERROR! File too big!
- Shout out to my EX for making room for something better to come into my life.
- Love is like a game, some people cheat and some prefer to play it fair.
- It's almost impossible to accept that the one you love, loves someone else.
- A relationship is like a job. You have to work hard to get it, and you have to work even harder to stay in it.
- With a right person, even a simple song will turn into a beautiful melody ♥

☞ Some people are meant to be in love with each other, but not meant to be together.

☞ Love is not about how much you say I love you, but how much you can prove that it's true.

☞ [I] shou[L]d be [OVE]r [YOU]

☞ True love is when you no longer want him/her, but you need them.

☞ Men are like mascara, they usually run at the first sign of emotion.

☞ Sometimes the feelings we start to have again are feelings that never really went away in the first place.

☞ Everything is so much funnier, when you have someone to laugh with.

☞ WARNING: The consumption of alcohol may lead you to believe that ex-lovers are really dying for you to telephone them at four in the morning.

☞ A zombie boyfriend will love you for your brain and not your body.

☞ The quickest way to get someone's attention is to no longer want it.

- ☞ Young love. Full of promise, full of hope. Ignorant of reality.
- ☞ It was love at first sight. Then I took a second look!!
- ☞ If you love someone set them free. Then send them a text message every hour letting them know you've set them free.
- ☞ If you cheat on someone that's willing to do anything for you, you actually cheated yourself.
- ☞ That amazing feeling when your crush texts you first.

MEN'S STATUS UPDATES

- Most women find me incredibly resistible.
- What does a burnt pizza, frozen beer, and a pregnant girl have in common? In each scenario there was a DUMBASS who didn't take it out in time.
- If you want a man's heart, go through his stomach. If you want his money, go through his pockets.
- Men are like lottery tickets. Very exciting at first, until you scratch away the surface to reveal the loser beneath.

- ☞ I have a devoted wife who lets me give it to her both ways...Cash or Credit.
- ☞ You know you're awesome when you can look at a photo on Facebook and say, "I have tagged that girl in more ways than one."
- ☞ Drinking beer like they need the cans back to make more.
- ☞ Men can read maps better than women. Only the male mind could conceive of one inch equaling a hundred miles.
- ☞ For guys, it doesn't matter whether we win or lose. We're going to lie about it anyway.
- ☞ Of course my clothes are on the floor. I'm a guy, that is where I hang them.
- ☞ If your dog is barking at the back door and your wife is yelling at the front door, who do you let in first? The dog, of course. He'll shut up once you let him in.
- ☞ I hope I'm the last guy on earth -- I want to see if all those women were lying to me.

- ☞ How many men does it take to open a beer? None. It should be opened by the time she brings it.
- ☞ Big sensitive guys cry, however, bigger guys laugh at that guy.
- ☞ Progress is made by lazy men looking for an easier way to do things.
- ☞ If a man is alone in the forest, and he says something, and there's no woman there to disagree with him, is he still wrong?
- ☞ You can easily judge the character of a man by how he treats those who can do nothing for him.
- ☞ At the beginning of a relationship, I wonder if women rub their hands together and say, "Let the games begin!"

WOMEN STATUS UPDATES

- ☞ Boys insult each other, but they really don't mean it. Girls compliment each other but they don't mean it either.
- ☞ For you men, who think a woman's place is in the kitchen, remember, that's where the knives are kept.
- ☞ Menstruation, menopause, mental breakdowns. Ever notice how all women's problems begin with men?
- ☞ The only reason why 30 guys liked your picture is because they can see right down your shirt.

- ☞ I'm not a bitch; I just have a low tolerance for bullshit.
- ☞ I like to pretend that I'm okay because I don't want to annoy people with my problems.
- ☞ GIRL please, I can remove 90% of your so-called "beauty" with a wet Kleenex!
- ☞ Admit it, we've all tried to splash water on our face like the commercials.
- ☞ Men know they have lost the fight as soon as we start crying.
- ☞ Women are like police, they can have all the evidence in the world but they still want a confession.
- ☞ The 3 fastest means of communication: Telephone, Television, Tell-a-woman.
- ☞ In a thousand years, archeologists will dig up tanning beds & think we fried people as punishments.
- ☞ Always believe a woman when she says: "You don't want to know!"
- ☞ Don't forget that women don't forget... anything.

- ☞ Women are angels, and when someone breaks our wings, we continue to fly... on a broomstick. We're flexible that way.
- ☞ Smiling is the best make up a girl can wear.
- ☞ What do I do when I see someone EXTREMELY GORGEOUS? I stare, I smile & when I get tired, I put the mirror down.
- ☞ Good girls are bad girls that never get caught.
- ☞ I have a theory that women don't fart, they hold it in until it comes out as drama.
- ☞ Got my hair done again. I'm so blonde now I can barely spell my last name.
- ☞ "I'm laying by the pool. Better take a picture of my legs and post it on the internet." – girls
- ☞ Women should not have children after 35. Really... 35 children are enough.
- ☞ We should put a jealous woman in charge of the FBI. They can uncover ANYTHING.

- ☞ The only one of your children who does not grow up and move away is your husband.
- ☞ If a girl destroys your house, keys your car, and tries to get you arrested, it's not love. She's crazy.
- ☞ If a girl compliments your dress, then you're wearing a pretty dress. If a guy compliments your dress, then you're wearing a slutty dress.
- ☞ Some girls need to chill with the make up. Your face is not a coloring book.
- ☞ Giving a girl the silent treatment is worse than actually cussing her out.
- ☞ Women like silent men. They think they're listening.

MISC. STATUS UPDATES

- LOL is the new way of saying "I really have nothing to say."
- Flies are everywhere, unfortunately the second I grab the fly swatter, they turn into ninjas.
- Duct tape is like "The Force." It has a light side and a dark side, and it holds the universe together.
- I don't make typos. I make new words.
- I turn down my radio to park my car.
- I have a hard time deciphering the fine line between boredom and hunger.

- ☞ I'd agree with you but then we would both be wrong.
- ☞ "Hi, may I help you?" "No I just waited 15 minutes in the line to say Hi."
- ☞ "I used to be the Internet!" - The Library
- ☞ Thought I was having deja-vu but it turns out I do the exact same things every day.
- ☞ Dear haters, I couldn't help but notice that "awesoME" ends with "me" and "Ugly" starts with "u."
- ☞ I'm not insulting you, I'm describing you!!
- ☞ When I say "the other day," it can mean any time up to a year ago.
- ☞ I'm not a stalker; I'm just bad with goodbyes.
- ☞ If it weren't for the last minute, nothing would get done.
- ☞ Even crime wouldn't pay if the government ran it.
- ☞ Some guy just gave me half of a peace sign.

- ☞ Telling someone that you're going to bed, when you're actually not, and then having to hold back from posting things on Facebook/Twitter.
- ☞ Random cash you discover in your pocket is the best.
- ☞ I'm a perfectionist when it comes to being imperfect.
- ☞ Hey couples who write on each other's Facebook walls, NO ONE cares how much you love each other, so cut it out!
- ☞ Be careful who you open up to. Only a few actually care, the rest are just curious.
- ☞ Dear clever comeback, can you come BEFORE the argument is over. Thanks!
- ☞ I'm staring at my closet full of clothes, but I have nothing to wear.
- ☞ Behind every ladybug there's a gentleman bug who is tired of dealing with her.
- ☞ Trying to sleep again thinking the dream will still continue.

- ☞ Not everyone's going to think I'm funny. Some people are going to think I'm hilarious.
- ☞ I don't understand banks. Why do they attach chains to their pens? If I trust you with my money, you should trust me with your pens.
- ☞ When I tell you, "It's a long story" it usually means I just don't want to tell you.
- ☞ I don't have a license to kill. I have a learner's permit.
- ☞ Thank you for reading this, I have officially wasted your time.
- ☞ Schizophrenia beats being alone.
- ☞ When you're home alone and you hear a strange noise & you're just like; ಠ_ಠ "WTF! WHO'S THERE?!"
- ☞ Morning radio shows exist to read the Internet to old people.
- ☞ Don't hate yourself in the morning. Sleep till noon.
- ☞ The past is a good place to visit, but definitely not a good place to stay.

- ☞ If the punch line to your joke or funny story is, "well, you had to be there," chances are it was never funny.
- ☞ Some people think the opposite of "Funny" is "Serious & Important." I think the real opposite of "Funny" is "Not Funny," like a bad sitcom.
- ☞ Mirrors don't lie. Lucky for you, they can't laugh either.
- ☞ Half of the world's misery comes from ignorance. The other half comes from intelligence.
- ☞ My misery likes tequila, not company.
- ☞ The future is that time when you'll wish you'd done what you aren't doing now.
- ☞ Help keep America beautiful. Stay in your house today.
- ☞ I generally don't approve of political jokes. I've seen too many of them get elected.
- ☞ My sleep number is "more, please."
- ☞ Know who doesn't want to be online right now? Fish.

☞ My room is not messy; it is an obstacle course designed to keep me fit.

☞ That was funny. But I don't like you. Therefore I shall not laugh.

☞ Funny how things change. I only want consistent friends NOT convenient friends.

☞ About 50% of the time "good luck" means "effff you."

☞ Why are there never any good side effects? Just once I'd like to see a drug commercial that says, May cause extreme awesomeness.

☞ Light travels faster than sound. This is why some people appear bright until you hear them speak.

☞ I don't have an attitude; I have a personality you can't handle.

☞ H.A.T.E.R.S. Having Anger Towards Everyone Reaching Success!!!

☞ We live in a society where pizza gets to your house before the police.

- ☞ Just because you have the right to do a thing does not mean you are right to do that thing.
- ☞ Just saw a T-shirt that said "by the time you're done reading this, I farted." Classic.
- ☞ Highway patrol officers must get sick of everyone driving the exact speed limit around them.
- ☞ Sometimes I make statements in the tone of a question?
- ☞ I'm fluent in three languages: English, Sarcasm, and Profanity.
- ☞ Turning off the downstairs lights and running upstairs so no one kills you.
- ☞ When I'm texting someone, I feel compelled to match that person's patterns of capitalization and punctuation.
- ☞ Adult: A person who has stopped growing at both ends and is now growing in the middle.
- ☞ Gee... When will the GIANT USED Car Tent Sale be back in town??? Said nobody, ever!

☞ I am noticing that the longer I live the more I see that I am never wrong about anything, and have only wasted my time in debating any issue.

☞ Better to remain silent and be thought a fool, than to speak and remove all doubt.

☞ You're good at giving advice, but not following your own.

☞ If swimming is great exercise, explain whales to me.

☞ Some people just need a pat, on the head, with a hammer.

☞ "You look tired" is just a polite way to tell someone they look like sh*t.

☞ Denial, anger, bargaining, depression, and acceptance...the 5 stages of me hitting the snooze button in the morning.

MOVIE / TELEVISION STATUS UPDATES

- "Who's that? What are they doing? What's happening?" – "Shut the hell up and watch the movie!"
- Some chick told me to get lost so I bought every season on DVD.
- I watch a scary movie, I'm perfectly fine, and then I go to bed and remember EVERY SINGLE SCARY MOMENT IN THE MOVIE.
- DiCaprio never died in Titanic... Last scene: going underwater. First scene of Inception is him waking up on a beach. IT'S A MOVIE INSIDE A MOVIE.

- If the people in the movies listened to me, they would still be alive.
- SPOILER: The whole Harry Potter saga turns out to be Harry's hallucination while he starves to death under the stairs in his abusive home.
- Comparing Twilight to Harry Potter is like comparing Rebecca Black to the Beatles.
- I hate waiting a whole week to see the next episode of my favorite show.
- Don't judge a book by its movie.
- When you pause a show and the people's faces look funny you can't help but laugh.
- If your movie is called Final Destination 5, it's probably not the final destination.
- Eating popcorn: 80% during the trailers. 20% during the movie.
- "You actually have friends?" "Yeah, all the 10 seasons on DVD!"
- Employee at Disney: Hey guys! I have a great idea! Instead of making new

movies, let's just remake the old ones in 3D!

- ☞ Question of the day: when was the last time that you saw a music video that was relevant to the actual song?

- ☞ When I watch MTV Cribs, I don't feel bad about downloading music illegally.

MUSIC & LYRICS STATUS UPDATES

- The fact that music can induce goosebumps, draw a tear, inspire, and connect is one of my favorite parts of being a human.
- Radio—making car rides less awkward since 1927.
- I hate when I'm making a milkshake & boys randomly show up in my yard.
- "That is THE dumbest song I've ever heard!" *2 weeks later* "This is my JAM!"

- ☞ When I'm in the car and a sad song comes on the radio, I stare out the window and act like I'm in a movie.

- ☞ My neighbors listen to some amazing music...whether they like it or not.

- ☞ OK, I'm going to admit it. It's been bugging me for about 10 years now and I need to get it off my chest. I let the dogs out.

- ☞ If I don't answer my phone, it's probably cause I am dancing to the ring tone.

- ☞ Musicians are always getting themselves in treble.

- ☞ If someday we all go to prison for downloading music, I just hope they split us up by the music genre.

- ☞ I'm going to start a band called "Free Beer" because when people see a sign that says "Free Beer Tomorrow at 9PM" everyone is going to be there.

- ☞ I dream of the day when my iTunes has only songs I LIKE!

- ☞ So vain. He probably thinks this status is about him.

- ☞ Q: What does Snoop Dogg do on Facebook? A: It's LIKE this and LIKE that.
- ☞ Is bringing sexy back... to the store for a refund.
- ☞ Imagine if Adele and Taylor Swift dated and then broke up.
- ☞ Moonwalking into jail, because you're a smooth criminal.
- ☞ I need music just as much as I need air.
- ☞ That awkward moment when Lady Gaga doesn't know what to wear for Halloween.

PHONE / SMS STATUS UPDATES

- RIGHT NOW YOU HAVE: 3 fingers behind your phone, your pinky tucked under for support and your scrolling with your thumb! LIKE if I'm right.
- I listen to nothing more closely than the muffled conversation happening after someone has accidentally butt dialed me.
- If I didn't have a laptop or cellphone, I'd go to bed at least 2 hours earlier every night.
- When you're walking then start texting and walk slower and slower and slower till you're just standing there, texting.

☞ I'm the type of person who laughs at my own texts before I send them, because I'm damn funny.

☞ My stupid phone doesn't have enough battery left to take any pictures, but it has enough battery to keep telling me that it's low.

☞ A morning text does not only mean, "Good Morning." It has a silent, loving message that says, "I think of you when I wake up."

☞ There really needs to be a 25-second UNDO on text messages.

☞ If you post a sideways picture, I have to assume you are a moron and don't know how to operate your phone or Facebook.

☞ Those contacts in your phone that you never talk/text but you never delete them.

☞ There's no panic like trying to press "End Call" when you make an accidental call.

☞ "Sending message failed, would you like to retry?" Well obviously...

☞ I hate when I miss a call by a few seconds, call the person back and they don't answer.

☞ I don't like that tone of voice you're texting me in.

- ☞ I only check my voicemail to get rid of that annoying little icon.
- ☞ I think it's funny how someone can update their status via mobile but can't text you back. Just saying.
- ☞ I should just change my voicemail greeting to: Please hang up and text me, thanks.
- ☞ If you text me first it's your job to make sure the conversation keeps going.
- ☞ I would walk one thousand miles just to talk to you... LOL, JK. I'm lazy, I'll text you.
- ☞ When I drop my phone, I act like I've dropped a newborn baby.
- ☞ Sorry about last night's texts. My phone was drunk.
- ☞ Arguing with auto-correct is the new yelling at the television.
- ☞ Do you make ninja moves you when you are about to drop your phone?
- ☞ Phones get thinner and smarter and people? We get fatter and stupid.
- ☞ Sending a risky text & thinking... "Oh, they hate me," if they don't respond within 30 seconds.

- Thanks to ringtones, I now associate all my favorite songs with the annoyance and dread of being interrupted and having to talk to somebody.
- Pretending to text in Awkward Situations.
- I'm pretty sure they had you in mind when they made the ignore button on my phone.
- Phone on silent. 10 missed calls. Turn volume to loudest. Nobody calls all day.
- That amazing moment when you drop your phone but the headphones save its life.
- If people could hear the next five seconds after I hit end on a call, I would have no friends.
- When I was young our phones didn't have Internet, they had SNAKE!
- One of the hardest things to do is trying to plug your phone into the charger when it's dark.
- When I'm bored nobody texts me. When I'm busy I'm the most popular person on the planet.
- If people winked in real life as much as they do in texts, the world would be a really creepy place.

RELATIONSHIP STATUS UPDATES

- ☞ When someone smells nice, it automatically makes them more attractive.

- ☞ Most relationships fail not because of absence of love; but because girls love too much & boys love too many.

- ☞ No one can promise they'll never hurt you, because at one time or another they will. The real promise is if the time you spent together will be worth the pain in the end.

- ☞ Relationships are like TATTOOS. They LOOK better than they FEEL.

- Grudges are a waste of perfect happiness. Laugh when you can, apologize when you should & let go of what you can't change.

- We ignore those who adore us, adore those who ignore us, love those who hurt us, and hurt those who love us.

- We fight like a married couple, talk like BFFs, flirt like first loves, & protect each other like siblings. Face it baby, we're meant to be.

- You can't have a relationship without any fights. But, you can make your relationship worth the fight.

- More relationships might survive if the partners realized that sometimes the better comes after the worse.

- My relationship status: ( ) Single ( ) In a Relationship ( ) Married ( ) Engaged ( ) Divorced (X) Waiting for a miracle.

- I don't want a perfect relationship. I just want someone who I can act silly with, someone who treats me well and loves being with me.

- ☞ If their ex is still calling...it's because they're still getting an answer.

- ☞ Trust is like an eraser, it gets smaller and smaller after every mistake.

- ☞ Everyone in life is going to hurt you, you just have to figure out which people are worth the pain.

- ☞ Some people come into your life as blessings, others come into your life as lessons.

- ☞ If you're single, focus on being a better you instead of looking for someone better than your ex. A better you will attract a better next.

- ☞ You always remember your first crush. Mine was Orange.

- ☞ A good relationship is with someone who knows all your insecurities, and imperfections and still loves you the same.

- ☞ "Hey, it's been forever. Let's hang out."
"No, it's been forever for a reason."

- ☞ Friends are forever, until they get into a relationship.

- We all have that ONE person that we always have feelings for no matter what. Just one look, and it takes you right back to that moment.

- The world is one big jigsaw puzzle. Only a few pieces fit together. If you should be lucky enough to find the piece that fits, don't let go!

- You need space?! JOIN NASA!

- You can't make the same mistake twice. The second time you make it, it's no longer a mistake, it's a choice.

- Sometimes the one you want is actually the one you're best without.

- Problem with girls; they love someone too much. Problem with boys; they let go too easily.

- I want a relationship that has a respectful, loyal, trustworthy, genuine commitment.

- Relationships don't need promises, terms, and conditions. They just need two wonderful people; one who can trust and one who can understand.

- ☞ They say couples should never go to bed angry. That's why married people always look so tired.

- ☞ The more I think about it, the more it pisses me off!

- ☞ "Single" and "In a relationship" are just terms people use. Your heart determines your status.

- ☞ I am not single, I'm romantically challenged.

- ☞ If you aren't happy being single, you'll never be happy in a relationship. Get your own life first, and then share it.

- ☞ If you can't make a simple question sound like an accusation, you're not qualified to be married.

- ☞ Teardrops = 1 percent water + 99 percent feelings.

- ☞ I'm not single; I'm in a long-term relationship with adventure & fun.

- ☞ Sometimes the right person for you was there all along. You just didn't see it because the wrong one was blocking the sight.

- Being replaced is one thing, not being missed is another.
- The nice thing about being single is, I'm always there when I need me.
- Relationships these days, start & end on Facebook.
- The minute I use a smiley in a conversation, I'm either bored, awkward or in love:)
- Our argument would be more impressive if either one of us knew what we were talking about.
- Every day, I think about texting you but then, I think "if you really wanted to talk to me, you'd text me first."
- If your relationship has more issues then your magazine, you need to cancel that subscription.
- I cannot be good enough for everyone, but I always try to be the best for the one who deserves me.
- Meeting men at bars is like window-shopping. You're looking at fancy clothes on a bunch of dummies.

- ☞ Facebook relationship status should have the option: "is getting played by_______"
- ☞ Nothing screams jealous insecure trust issues louder than a joint Facebook profile.
- ☞ Single doesn't mean lonely. Single means you're preparing for the arrival of a BETTER love!!!
- ☞ There are over 7,000,000,000 people on this earth. Don't let 1 bring you down.
- ☞ Sometimes, when one person is missing, the whole world seems depopulated.
- ☞ I don't need a certain number of friends, just a number of friends I can be certain of.
- ☞ It's not always the tears that measure the pain. Sometimes it's the smile we fake.
- ☞ There are some people in life that make you laugh a little louder, smile a little bigger and live just a little bit better.
- ☞ "We have a history," sounds a lot better than "we used to hook-up and now it's awkward."

- ☞ When choosing a path in life, try to avoid the psychopaths.
- ☞ Tired of being single? Go sleep on the couch for a night and remember what it feels like to be in a relationship.
- ☞ No I am not single. I am in a long distance relationship. My significant other lives in the future.
- ☞ Marriage is like a late night phone call. You get a ring and then you wake up.
- ☞ Marriage changes passion…suddenly you're in bed with a relative.
- ☞ Not looking at my phone during dinner will be the most romantic gesture I will make today.
- ☞ My wife and I always hold hands. If I let go, she shops.
- ☞ Are you supposed to get an email that says "HAHAHAHAHA" after signing up for Match.com?
- ☞ I hope I never meet the girl of my dreams. She's seen me in a lot of awkward situations.

- ☞ Always tell your significant other the truth—the carefully edited truth.
- ☞ Give me an awkward morning over any lonely night.
- ☞ Marriage is about give and take. You better give it to her or she'll take it anyway.
- ☞ By the time a man realizes that his father was right, he has a son who thinks he's wrong.
- ☞ I wish relationships were more like cell phone plans - free nights and weekends.
- ☞ Looking at your ex and wondering "was I drunk the entire relationship?"

SCHOOL STATUS UPDATES

- ☞ There will be always that one teacher asking you a question and your friend next to you whispering the answer.
- ☞ The best 2 days of school are always the first and the last.
- ☞ True friends are always there for you. Fake friends only appear when they want something from you.
- ☞ Teacher: Whoever answers my next question can go home. *Boy throws bag out the window* Teacher: Who threw that? Boy: Me, I'm going home.

- When your teacher says, "get out" it means you won the argument.
- C.L.A.S.S- Come Late And Start Sleeping.
- My friends don't care if my room is messy. They only care if I have food at my house.
- Dude, I said you could borrow my pen, not chew it like it's a toy.
- If we learn by our mistakes, some of us are getting one great education!
- I do my homework for a while then I reward myself a short break. The funny thing is that the break is never short.
- I don't need sleeping pills. I have BOOKS.
- If Twitter & Facebook were school subjects my parents would be so proud of me.
- Even when I have absolutely nothing to do, I still don't do my homework.
- Judging by my handwriting, possible future career choices include doctor or kindergartner.

- ☞ How come the bus driver is the only one with a seatbelt?
- ☞ Doing the "I'm thinking really hard face" when the teacher looks at you.
- ☞ Hey Google, why do you not sit next to me during my exam?
- ☞ Teacher: Why can I hear talking? Student: Because you have ears.
- ☞ "Class, I couldn't grade your papers. I was busy." Ummm Yah... I couldn't do my homework. I'm busy too.
- ☞ I die a little inside when I see the word "explain" on a test.
- ☞ A friend isn't someone who is nice to your face; it's someone who isn't rude to you behind your back.
- ☞ In school, the only thing group projects ever taught me was that I hate other people.
- ☞ Tired apostrophes risk falling into a comma.
- ☞ Sometimes I think life is one big test and I'm in the wrong classroom.

SILLY STATUS UPDATES

- That fake laugh you do when you don't understand what somebody just said to you.

- I was watching the advertisement commercial for Snuggies, which I think is an incredibly stupid invention. Then I wanted to change the channel, but I couldn't reach the remote because my arm was under a blanket and I didn't want to remove it because my arm was cold.

- Nothing sucks more than that moment during an argument when you realize you're wrong.

- ☞ Is it rude to throw a breath mint in someone's mouth while they are talking?

- ☞ Why do we use our blankets as shields at night? Is the monster going to be like, "Oh crap. They have a blanket... RRRUUUUNNN!!!!"

- ☞ I don't hate you; I'm just not necessarily excited about your existence.

- ☞ Mind Melter: Why is there a "D" when it's a Fridge. But, not when it's a refrigerator?

- ☞ Try to say the letter "M" without your lips touching.

- ☞ If the cops arrest a mime, do they tell him he has the right to remain silent?

- ☞ When I was born, I was so surprised, that's why I didn't talk for a year and a half.

- ☞ I'm painting a blue square in the backyard... so Google Earth thinks I have a pool.

- ☞ It's not denial. I'm just selective about the reality I accept.

☞ How come when I wake myself up from talking in my sleep, I feel its necessary to finish the conversation out loud?

☞ Sometimes I don't even know when I'm being sarcastic.

☞ I'm not trying to impress you or anything, but... I'm Batman!

☞ Dear Thursday, Move out of the freaking way. Sincerely Friday.

☞ Cul-de-sac is what rich people call a dead end.

☞ The leading cause of death in mice is scientists.

☞ Don't look now, but I'm hiding under your bed.

☞ So I've narrowed it down and I'm either going to start a motorcycle gang or take a nap.

☞ I'm going to open a restaurant and call it "I Don't Care"...so us men can finally take you women to the place you want to go when we ask.

- ☞ FUN FACT: All kitties share a common ancestor, whose name was "Snickerboots Fancybasket."

- ☞ I watch pom. You probably misread that. LIKE if you did.

- ☞ They should call the lobby of any IRS office Formville.

TRAVEL STATUS UPDATES

- The USA is like a dysfunctional family... We're pretty messed up but, we still love each other.

- Where do women pee? Cause all I ever see on signs is Men and Scottish Men.

- I walk the streets with a smile on my face while looking up just in case the cameras of Google Maps are filming.

- Go to Google Maps, bring up directions from Washington D.C. to Japan and look at instruction number 48.

☞ I can't wait till 2013 so I can laugh at everyone who thought the world was going to end in 2012.

☞ You're not an American until you've eaten more than the serving suggestion.

☞ The problem with America is stupidity. I'm not saying there should be a capital punishment for stupidity, but why don't we just take the safety labels off of everything and let the problem solve itself?

☞ I love airports. They're pretty much the only place besides a tailgate where it's acceptable to drink at 9am.

☞ When I turn on my blinker, I'm not asking permission-I'm warning you.

☞ You are never fully dressed until you wear a smile.

VIDEO GAME STATUS UPDATES

- No, I'm not feeling violent; I'm feeling creative with weapons.
- Remember when you had to go to channel 3 to play video games?
- I have a feeling these birds wouldn't be so angry if we'd stop sling-shooting them thru the air.
- It's 2012 and we're not driving dragons? The future sickens me.
- Some people worry about actual real problems and others worry about a virtual farm.

- I'm sad because I don't have an Xbox. Someone console me.
- Law of Online Gaming: Anybody that's worse than you is a n00b. Anybody that's better than you has no life.
- My girlfriend left me because of my video game addiction. I guess Wii didn't Kinect.
- Life is like Mario Bros you have to slay a lot of dragons before you meet your Princess.

WORK/CAREER STATUS UPDATES

- "Okay, just going to check Facebook ONE MORE TIME and then I'll get back to work." – me, always

- Closing all the Internet windows by the time your boss gets to your desk is like getting the keys into the door before the killer gets you.

- Is there a mouse that doesn't make a clicking noise as I'm trying to close 10 windows when my boss walks into my office?

- I hate how my job always expects me to show up.

- ☞ I yawn all day at work & school. But when it comes to the night, I'm not tired at all.
- ☞ Don't think of yourself as a failure, think of yourself as unspoiled by success.
- ☞ Hating everything saves countless hours of decision-making.
- ☞ Paperclip: the staple for people with commitment issues.
- ☞ Confession is good for the soul but bad for your career.
- ☞ Giving co-workers the silent treatment by sending them blank emails.
- ☞ Rich people have big libraries. Poor people have big TVs.
- ☞ Do not argue with an idiot. He will drag you down to his level and beat you with experience.
- ☞ If you don't have any critics, you probably don't have any success either!
- ☞ Work through lunch? I don't even work through work.
- ☞ If boredom were a career, I'd be at the top of my field!

- ☞ When I "rage against the machine" the machine is usually a printer.
- ☞ When impersonating a coworker, I like to add a little extra dumb to their voice.
- ☞ Business conventions are important because they demonstrate how many people a company can operate without.
- ☞ Experience is what you get when you didn't get what you wanted.
- ☞ Hard work is the single greatest competitive advantage. Ideas don't happen because they are great.
- ☞ Funny how fast you can get up in the morning once you've realized you overslept.
- ☞ Not taking risks is risky.
- ☞ I'm on hold. My call is important to them.
- ☞ Hard work never hurt anybody. But I'm hoping the boss will be first.
- ☞ Worrying works! 90% of the things I worry about never happen.

- ☞ Some people say I'm a dreamer, others say, "If you fall asleep at work again we're going to have to let you go."
- ☞ It's the little things in life that count. Like my salary.
- ☞ A bus station is where a bus stops. A train station is where a train stops. On my desk, I have a work station.
- ☞ My coworkers are exceptionally dedicated. You wouldn't believe how far some of them will go to annoy me.
- ☞ I thought I wanted a career, turns out I just wanted paychecks.
- ☞ I like work. It fascinates me. I sit and look at it for hours.
- ☞ The trouble with being punctual is that nobody's there to appreciate it.
- ☞ It's not how good your work is, it's how well you explain it.
- ☞ If you do a job too well, you will get stuck with it.
- ☞ Banging your head against a wall uses 150 calories/hr.

- ☞ I always try to go the extra mile at work, but my boss always finds me and brings me back.
- ☞ The most ineffective workers are systematically moved to the place where they can do the least damage: Management.
- ☞ Do you want to speak to the manager or someone who knows what's going on?
- ☞ If you ever get caught sleeping on the job, slowly raise your head and say... Amen.

DID YOU KNOW: If you text "LIKE FUNNYSTATUSUPDATE" to FBOOK (32665) you'll LIKE our Fan Page :) Find out what else you can do via SMS Text Message on Facebook @ www.facebook.com/mobile/texts.php

5 LITTLE KNOWN FACEBOOK FACTS

1. You can see what Facebook employees are eating by going to: www.facebook.com/FacebookCulinaryTeam. They've been known to eat such things as "Bacon-Wrapped Hot Dogs & Thin-Mints for dessert."

2. A Facebook Employee Hoodie once sold on the auction website eBay for $4,000+

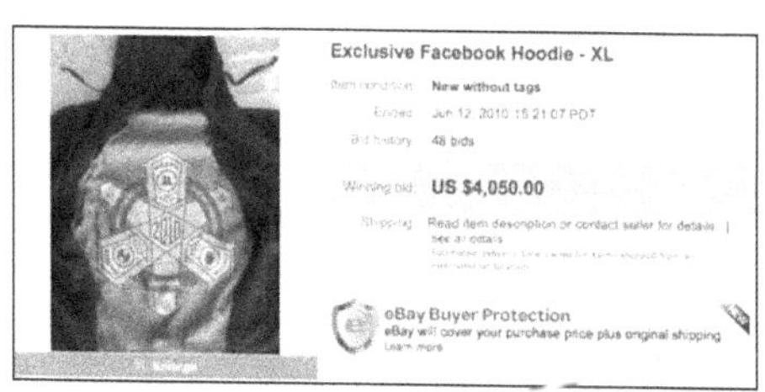

3. If you go to Facebook.com/4 it takes you to the Timeline of Mark Zuckerberg (co-founder of Facebook).

4. Adding the numbers 5 or 6 to the end of the URL will take you to the respective profiles of Chris Hughes and Dustin Moskovitz, Facebook co-founders and Mark's former college roommates. Tacking a 7 onto the web address leads to the profile of Arie Hasit, a good friend of Zuckerberg's, from his days at Harvard.

5. Al Pacino's Face appeared on the original masthead for Facebook's website.

6. Facebook was initially bank-rolled with a $500,000 investment by Peter Thiel, the co-founder of Paypal.

Additional Resources:

- ☞ FunnyStatus.com
- ☞ http://en.wikipedia.org/wiki/Facebook
- ☞ https://blog.facebook.com/

LEGAL STUFF

Facebook® is a registered trademark of Facebook, Inc.

This book is not affiliated with Facebook.

This book was created as a work of humor and is intended for entertainment purposes only. This book makes no claim or guarantee to any of the content within. Again, this book is for entertainment purposes only.

The content included herein is user-generated, from submissions to **www.funnystatus.com.**

How can you use this book?

MOTIVATE

EDUCATE

THANK

INSPIRE

PROMOTE

CONNECT

Why have a custom version of *Funny Status Updates for Facebook*?

- Build personal bonds with customers, prospects, employees, donors, and key constituencies
- Develop a long-lasting reminder of your event, milestone, or celebration
- Provide a keepsake that inspires change in behavior and change in lives
- Deliver the ultimate "thank you" gift that remains on coffee tables and bookshelves
- Generate the "wow" factor

Books are thoughtful gifts that provide a genuine sentiment that other promotional items cannot express. They promote employee discussions and interaction, reinforce an event's meaning or location, and they make a lasting impression. Use your book to say "Thank You" and show people that you care.

Funny Status Updates for Facebook is available in bulk quantities and in customized versions at special discounts for corporate, institutional, and educational purposes. To learn more please contact our Special Sales team at:

1.866.775.1696 • sales@advantageww.com • www.AdvantageSpecialSales.com